D0578733

# GOING HOME

Margaret Wild • Wayne Harris

SCHOLASTIC INC.
New York

To Donna. MW
To Mary Mellis. WH

 Published by Scholastic Inc.,
555 Broadway, New York, NY 10012.
by arrangement with Ashton Scholastic.


Library of Congress Cataloging-in-Publication Data

Wild, Margaret, 1948–
Going home / by Margaret Wild; illustrations by Wayne Harris.
p. cm.
Summary: While waiting to leave the hospital, Hugo dreams of
adventures with exotic animals in faraway lands.
ISBN 0-590-47958-X
[1. Hospitals — Fiction. 2. Dreams — Fiction. 3. Voyages and
travels — Fiction.] I. Harris, Wayne, ill. II. Title.
PZ7.W64574Go 1994 93-22975
[E] — dc20 CIP
AC

12 11 10 9 8 7 6 5 4 3 2 4 5 6 7 8 9/9

Printed in the U.S.A.

The illustrations for this book
were painted with acrylics.

First Scholastic printing, April 1994

Hugo is in a small hospital
right next to the zoo.
He's much better and wants
to go home.
"Soon," says the doctor.
But how soon is soon?

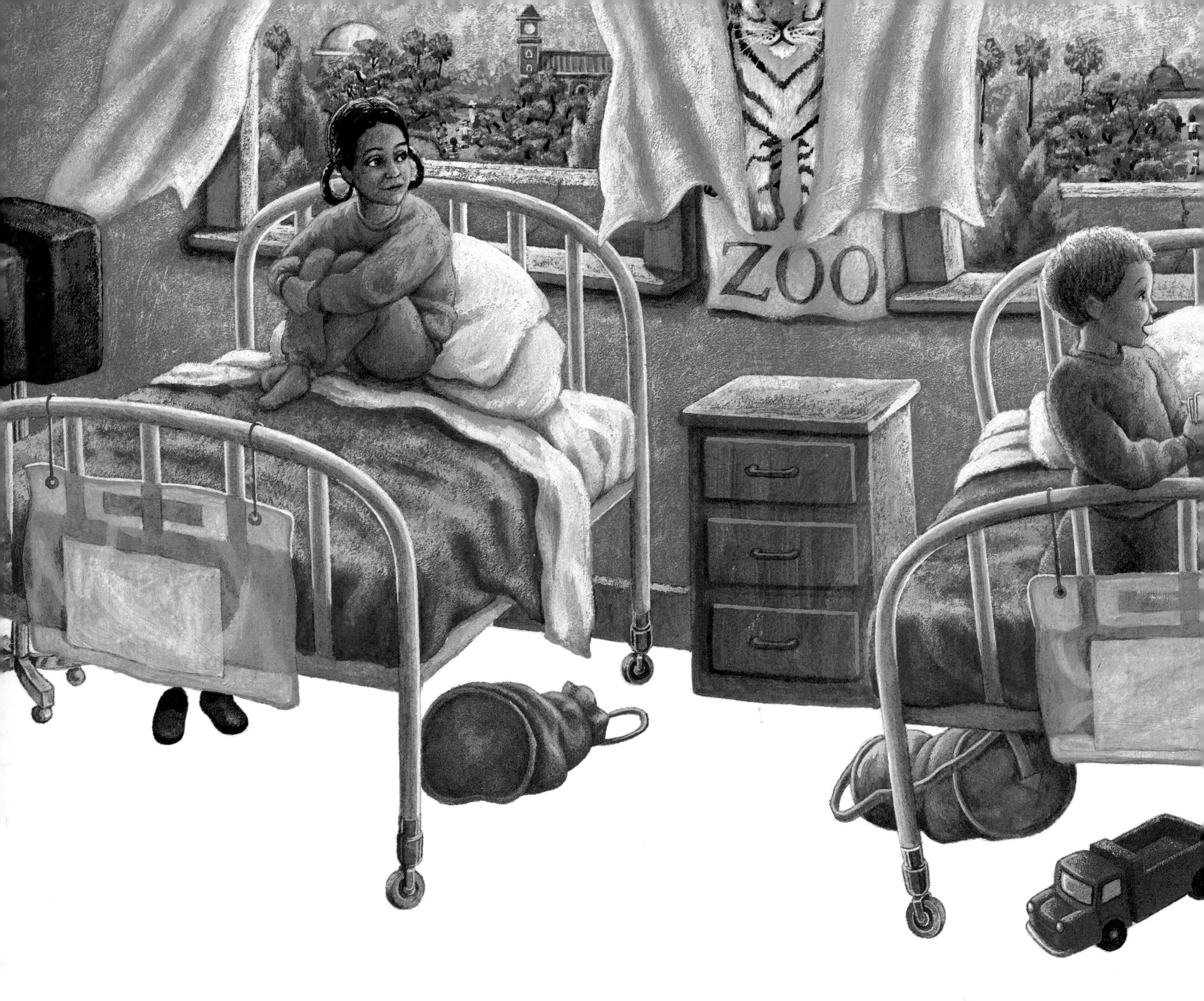


"Cheer up. It won't be long now," says Nurse Benny.

"Come and play cards," says Simon in the next bed.

"This is a really good show," says Nirmala, who watches TV all the time.

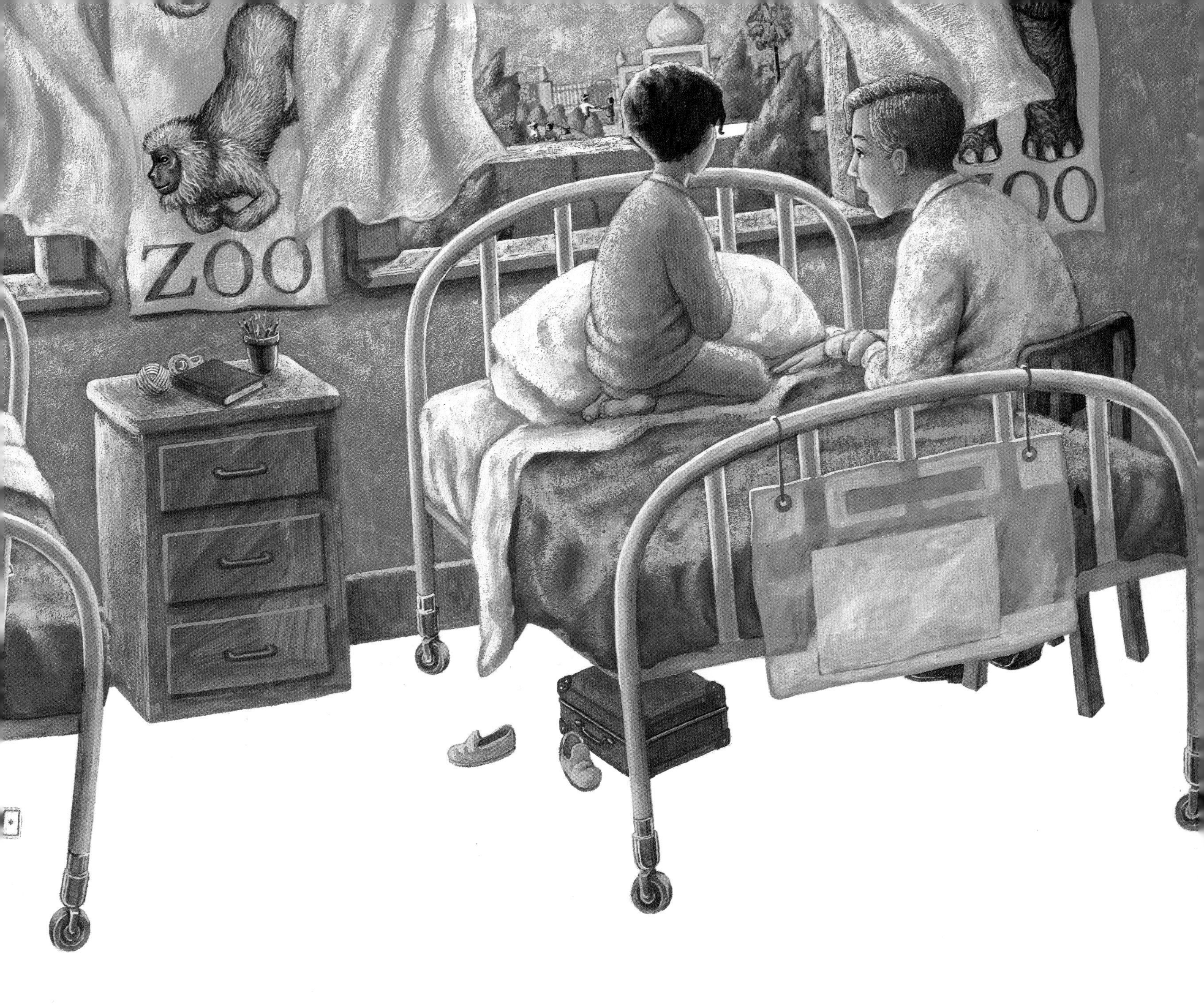


But Hugo shakes his head and stares out the window. Right now Mom will be putting on the kettle, and his little sister, Cathy, will be playing dress-up, and his fat cat, Lucy, will be napping in the sun.

So Hugo stares out the window,
listening to the animal noises
that float up from the zoo.
"What a racket," says Nurse Benny,
but Hugo's eyes widen because an
elephant is shrieking something
special — a message just for him.

"Come, come home with me," shrieks the elephant.
So Hugo puts on his slippers — and goes.
He and the elephant amble through African grasslands,
where lions play rough-and-tumble games, and herds
of wildebeests migrate across the plains.

When his family comes to visit,
Mom asks as usual,
"What have you been up to?"

"Quite a lot," says Hugo.
"I went to Africa."

"Lucky you," says Mom.

"It's not fair!" says Cathy.
"I only went to kindergarten."

So Hugo makes her a little paper
elephant with flappy ears.

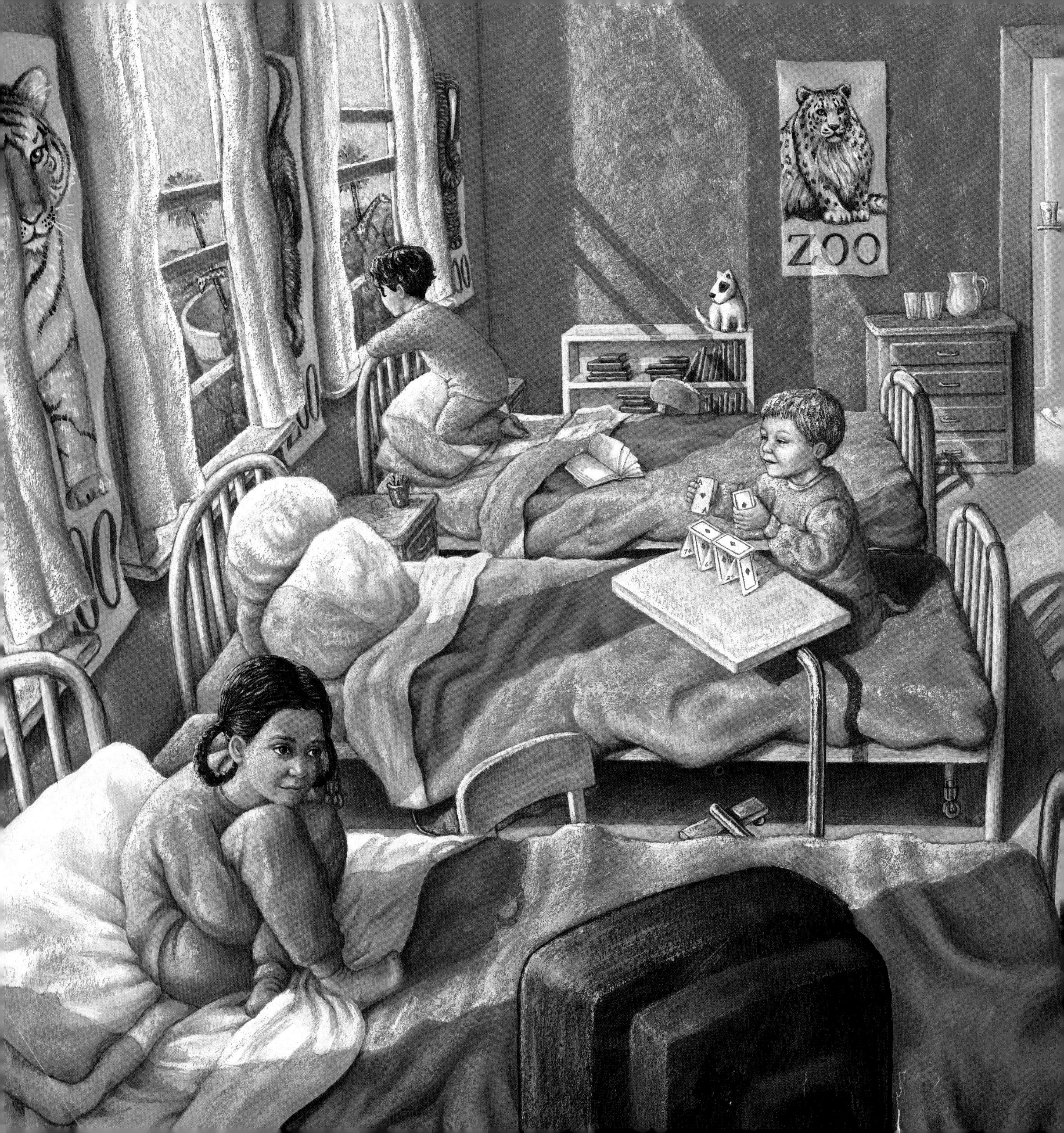
ZOO

The next day while Simon is building a house out of cards and Nirmala is still watching TV, Hugo stares out the window and listens again.

The elephant is silent,
but the howler monkey is roaring,
"Come, come home with me."
So Hugo puts on his slippers — and goes.

He and the howler monkey swing through the treetops of the Amazon jungle, where sloths sleep upside down, and the emerald tree boa hides in the leaves, and toucans gobble berries.

When his family comes to visit, Mom asks,
"Where did you go today?"

"Quite far," says Hugo.
"I went to the Amazon jungle."

"Lucky, lucky you," sighs Mom.

"It's not fair!" says Cathy.
"I only went to the corner shop."

So Hugo makes her a monkey puppet
that wiggles on her finger.

The next day, after Hugo has
played cards with Simon and
watched a bit of TV with Nirmala,
he stares out the window.
And, very faintly, he can hear
the snow leopard growling,
"Come, come home with me."
So Hugo puts on his slippers
— and goes.

He wraps his arms around
the snow leopard's neck, and they
hurtle through snow and ice
high in the Himalayas,
where eagle-eyed birds soar
above the slopes.

When his family comes to visit,
Mom asks, "Been traveling again?"

"Yes," says Hugo,
"I went to the Himalayas."

Cathy stamps her foot. "Not fair!
I only went to the park."

So Hugo makes her a leopard
mask, and she growls and shows
her claws.

ZOO

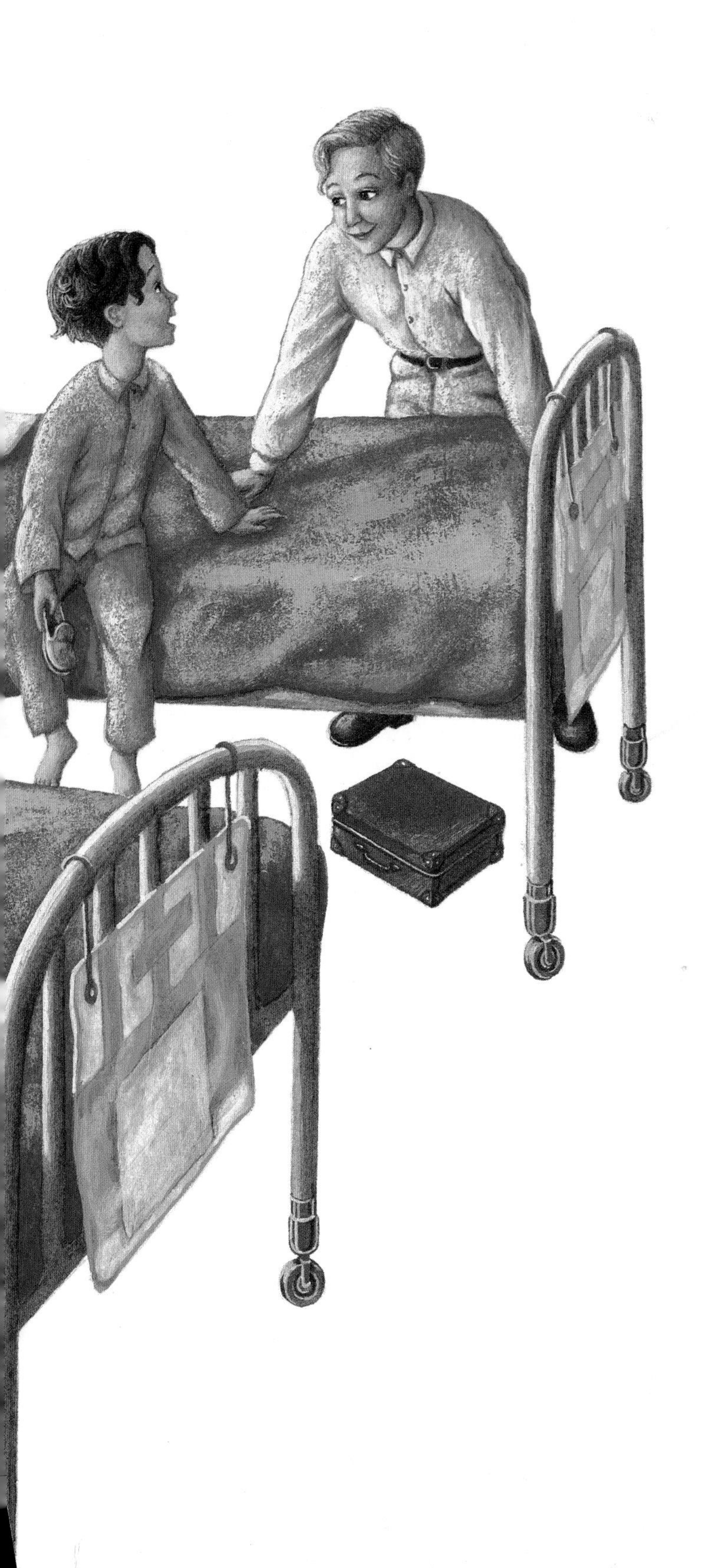

The next day when Hugo is just about to put on his slippers and leave for India, Nurse Benny says, "Surprise! Your mom and Cathy are here — you're going home."

"Come back and visit me," says Simon.

"I wish I were going home, too," says Nirmala, and she watches TV harder than ever.

"I'll tell you both a secret," says Hugo,
and he whispers in their ears.

ZOO

That night when Hugo is snuggled up
in his own bed in his own house at last . . .

Nirmala and Simon put on their slippers . . .

and run with the tiger
through the forests of India.